10,000 Maniacs

Amsco Publications
New York/London/Sydney

Cover design by Frank Olinsky and Miss Merchant
Photography by Rob Marinissen
Music arrangements by David Pearl

Order No. AM 91046
International Standard Book Number: 0.8256.1350.7

Exclusive Distributors:
Music Sales Corporation
225 Park Avenue South, New York, NY 10003 USA

Printed in the United States of America by
Vicks Lithograph and Printing Corporation

Contents

Noah's Dove

Merchant

Am Dm G

lieved it. I nev - er felt cheat - ed.

Am Em F C

You were the___ cho - sen one,
In that___ Au - gust breeze

Am Em F

the pure___ eyes of___ No - ah's___
of those for - got - ten___

C Dm Am

dove. Choir boys___ and an - gels
trees, your time was set___ for leav - ing,

Dm
G
stole your lips and your ha - lo.
come a cold - er sea - son.
In your reck - less
C
Dm
Am
G
mind, you act as if you've got more lives.
In your reck - less
mf
C
Dm
Am
Dm
eyes,
you on - ly have time and your love of dan -
it's nev - er too late for a chance to seize
Am
1. Dm
G
ger — to it you're no stran - ger
some

2.
Dm
G
fin - al breath of free - dom.
Am
Em
Ve
R.H.
G
C
Am
ry,
so ve - ry wise.
Em

F
C
Am
Em
F
C
Don't re - veal it. I'm
Dm
Am
tired, tired of know - ing
Dm
G
where it is you're go - ing. In your reck - less

C Dm Am G

mind, you act as if you've got more lives. In your reck - less

f

C Dm Am Dm

eyes, { you on - ly have time and your ___ love of dan -
{ it's nev - er too late for a ___ chance to seize ___

Am 1. Dm G

ger ___ to it you're no stran - ger. In your reck - less
___ some

2. Dm G

fi - nal breath of free - dom.

These Are Days

BUCK/MERCHANT

A (B♭) — G (A♭) — D (E♭)

world be warm as this. And as you feel it.
mir - a - cles you see in ev - ery hour.

A (B♭) — G (A♭) — D/F♯ (E♭/G)

you'll know it's true that you are
you'll know it's true that you are

G5 (A♭5) — A5 (B♭5) — G (A♭)

blessed and luck - y. It's true that
blessed and luck - y. It's true that

1.

D/F♯ (E♭/G) — G5 (A♭5) — A5 (B♭5)

you are touched by some - thing that will grow and bloom

G
A♭
D
E♭
G/D
A♭/E♭
in you.
D
E♭
Asus4
B♭sus4
2. D/F♯
E♭/G
G
A♭
D/F♯
E♭/G
Em
Fm
D
E♭
you are touched by some - thing
A
B♭
G
A♭
D
E♭
that - 'll grow and bloom in you.
G/D
A♭/E♭
D
E♭
These

D
G/D
D
A
E♭
A♭/E♭
E♭
B♭
are
days.
These are
the days you might fill with laugh - ter un - til you
G
A♭
D/F♯
E♭/G
break.
These days you might feel a shaft of light make its way
A
B♭
across your face.
And when you do,
you'll know

D/F♯
E♭/G
G
A♭
how it was meant to be. See the signs, know their mean - ing.
A
B♭
G
A♭
D/F♯
E♭/G
It's true, you'll know how it was meant to be.
G
A♭
A
B♭
G
A♭
Hear the signs and know they're speak - ing to you, to you.
D
E♭
G/D
A♭/E♭
D
E♭
Asus4
B♭sus4
Repeat and fade

Eden

Buck/Drew/Gustafson
Augustyniak/Merchant

Fsus2
C/E
Fsus2
ros - es in the gar - den, beau - ty with thorns a - mong our
C/E
Fsus2
C/E
leaves. To pick a rose you ask your hands
Gsus4
Fsus2
to bleed. What is the rea - son for hav - ing ros -
C/E
Fsus2
C/E
es when your blood is shed care - less - ly?

Fsus2 C/E C

It must be for some - thing more than

Am Fsus2 C/E

van - i - ty.

Fsus2 C/E Fsus2

Ooh.

C/E C Am

Be - lieve me, the

Fsus2
C/E
Fsus2
truth is we're not ho - nest, not the peo - ple that we
C/E
Fsus2
C/E
dream. We're not as close as we could be.
Gsus4
Fsus2
Wil - ling to grow but rains are shal -
C/E
Fsus2
C/E
low. Bar - ren and wind - scat - tered seed

Fsus2
C/E
Gsus4
on stone and dry land, we will
Fsus2
C/E
be. Wait - ing for the light a - ris - en to
Fsus2
C/E
Fsus2
flood in - side the pri - son.
C/E
Gsus4
And in that time kind

Fsus2
C/E
Fsus2
words a - lone will teach us, no bit - ter - ness will reach
C/E
Fsus2
C/E
us. Rea - son will be guid - ed
C
Am
Fsus2
in a - no - ther way.
C/E
Fsus2
C/E
Ooh.

Fsus2
C/E
C
Am
Fsus2
C/E
Fsus2
C/E
Fsus2
C/E
Gsus2
All in time,
but the

Fsus2
C/E
Fsus2
clock is a - no - ther de - mon that de - vours our time in
eyes see well be - neath us, flow - ers all di -
C/E
Fsus2
1. C/E
E - den, in our Par - a -
vine?
Gsus4
2. C/E
dise. Will our
Gsus4
Fsus2
Is there still time? If we wake and dis -

C/E
Fsus2
C/E
cov - er in life a prec - ious love,
Fsus2
C/E
Gsus4
will that wak - ing be - come more
Am
heav - en - ly?
C
Ee.

Few and Far Between

MERCHANT

D/F♯
Am7
upon our lives without regret. Of all the
a future. I swear by what I say. What-e-ver
D
things I have done you think I'm proud of ev-'ry one
pen-ance you'll do, de-cide what it's worth to you
1.
C
without exception?
2.
and then re-
C
spect it. How-ev-er
D
long it will take

to wea - ther your mis - takes why not ac -
3
3
C
Am
Em
cept it?
My hands, for now, are tied.
C
Am
I'm a bod - y fro - zen. I'm a
Em
C
will that's par - a - lyzed.
When will you ev - er

G
x000
D/F♯
x0 x
Am7
x0 0 0
set a - side your pain and mis - er - y?
G
x000
D/F♯
x0 x
No mat - ter how I beg, no mat - ter how I wish or
Am7
x0 0 0
D
xx0
plead, you'll ne - ver be more than a - live.
You'll ne - ver do more than sur - vive un - til you ex -

C
Am
Em
D
pect it.
Do you want to build a world with our lives?
You bet-ter soon de-cide or you can for-
get it.
My hands, for now, are tied.
I'm a bod-y fro-zen. I'm a

Em
C
will that's par - a - lyzed.
Till you
Am
Em
C
drop that heav - y bag - gage you're drag - ging be - hind,
Am
Em
there won't be room for us to both go
C
G
this ride.

Stockton Gala Days

BUCK/DREW/GUSTAFSON
AUGUSTYNIAK/MERCHANT

Csus4
where.
hair.
Em - er - ald green
Blue in the stream
(3.) Vio - let ser - ene
like none I have
F
Bb
F
seen a - part of dreams that es - cape me.
Bb
F
Csus4
There was no girl as
warm
bold
warm
as you.
Bb
F
How I've learned to please, to

B♭
F
B♭
doubt my - self in need,
you'll nev - er,
F
Csus4
1.
you'll ne - ver know.
2. That sum - mer
2.
Dm
You'll nev - er know.
3.
How

Bb
F
Bb
I've learned to please, to doubt my - self in need.
F
Bb
F
You'll nev - er, you'll nev - er know.
Csus4
Dm
You'll nev - er know.

Csus4
F
That sum-mer fields grew high. We had
Bb
F
Bb
wild - flow - er fe - ver. We had to
F
Csus4
lay down where they grew. (Where they grew.) How I've
F
Bb
learned to hide, how I've locked in - side, you'd be sur - prised if shown.

F
B♭
F
But you'll nev - er, you'll nev - er
Csus4
know.
1.
2.
How I've
C/G
Dm
poco rit.

Gold Rush Brides

BUCK/MERCHANT

C/E
C
G/B
Am
C
the talk - ing wire from where to who knows?
G7sus4/D
F
C
There's no
F
C/E
way to di - vide the beau - ty of the sky from the
home - stead wives? Who were the gold rush brides?
mp
C
G/B
Am
C
F
wild west - ern plains. Where a man could drift, in leg -
Does an - y - bod - y know? Do their works sur - vive their yel -

C/E
C
G/B
Am
C
end - ar - y myth, by roam - ing o - ver spac - es.
low fe - ver lives in the pa - ges they wrote?
G7sus4/D
F
C
The land was
The land was
G7sus4/D
F
free and the price was right.
free, yet it cost their lives.
mf
C
Gm
Da - ko - ta on the wall is a
In min - er's lust for gold a fam - ily's

F
C
Gm
F
C
Gm
F
C
1.
white - robed wo - man broad yet maid - en - ly. Such
house was bought and sold, piece by piece. A
pow - er in her hand as she hails the wa - gon man's fam -
wid - ow staked her claim on a dol - lar and his name, so pain -
i - ly. I see In - di - ans that crawl through this
ful - ly. In let - ters mailed back home her East - ern
mu - ral that re - calls our his - tor - y. Who were the
sis - ters they would moan as they would read

2.
Gm
F
ac - counts of mad - ness, child - birth, lone - li - ness and
C
Gm
grief.
Ac - counts of mad - ness, child -
F
C
birth, lone - li - ness and grief.
Gm
F
C

Circle Dream

BUCK/DREW/GUSTAFSON
AUGUSTYNIAK/MERCHANT

Csus4
C
Csus4
cle round.
I dreamed of a cir - cle,
C
Csus4
Dm
C/E
I dreamed of a cir - cle round.
And in that
G/D
G
Dm
C/E
G/D
G
cir - cle I had made
were all the worlds un - formed
and un -
simile
C
Dm7
G
born yet.
A vol - ume, a sphere

Dm7
G
C
that was the earth, that was the moon,
G/D
G
G/D
C
that did re - volve a - round my room.
Csus4
C
Csus4

C
Csus4
C
I dreamed of a cir - cle, I dreamed of a cir -
(I dreamed of a cir - cle.)
p
Csus4
Dm
C/E
G/D
G
cle round. And in that cir - cle was a maze,
And in that cir - cle was a face.
simile
Dm
C/E
G/D
G
C
a ter - ri - ble spi - ral to be lost in.
Her eyes looked up - on me with fond - ness.
Dm7
G
Dm7
G
Blind in my fear, I was es - cap - ing just
Her warmth com - ing near, call - ing me "sweet - ness," call -

C
G/D
G
by feel.
ling me "dear."
But at ev - ery turn,
But I whis-pered, "no,
G/D
C
Csus4
my way was sealed.
I can't rest here."
C
Csus4
C
I dreamed of a
p
Csus4
C
Csus4
C
cir - cle. I dreamed of a cir - cle round..( )
(I dreamed of a cir - cle.)

How You've Grown

MERCHANT

B♭ F/A Gm7

mem-ber those words and how they chid - ed me, when

B♭ F/A Gm7

pa - tient was the hard - est thing to be.

C Dm F

Be - cause we can't make up for the time that we've

mp

C Dm B♭ F/A

lost, I must let these mem-o - ries pro - vide.

Gm7sus4
B♭
F/A
No lit - tle girl can stop the world to wait for me.
Gm7
stronger beat
F
to Coda
Gm7
I should have known. At your
mf
B♭
F/A
Gm7
age in a string of days the year is gone. But
B♭
F/A
Gm7
D.S. al Coda
in that space of time, it takes so long.

Coda

F Gm7 B♭ Csus4

Ev-'ry-time we say good-bye you're fro-zen in my mind as the

mf

Dm Csus4 B♭ F/A

child that you ne-ver will be, you ne-ver will be a-

Gm7 F Gm7

gain.

Instrumental solo

B♭ F/A Gm7 Csus4 C

Dm
F
C
Dm
B♭
F/A
Gm7sus4
I'll ne - ver be
be
B♭
F/A
Gm7
more to you than a stran - ger could be.
F
Gm7
B♭
Csus4
Ev - 'ry - time we say good - bye
you're fro - zen in my mind as the

Dm
Csus4
B♭
F/A
child that you ne - ver will be,
you ne - ver will be a -
Gm7
F
Gm7
gain.
Ev - 'ry - time we say good - bye
B♭
Csus4
Dm
Csus4
you're fro - zen in my mind as the child that you ne - ver will be,
B♭
F
will be a - gain.
poco rit.

Candy Everybody Wants

DREW/MERCHANT

F♯m7
Gm7
D
E♭
dy, if blood and love taste so sweet, then
A
B♭
we give 'em what they want.
F♯m7
Gm7
Dadd9
E♭add9
Hey,
A
B♭
hey, give 'em what they want.

A/C♯
Bb/D
D
Eb
So their eyes are grow - ing haz - y
Esus4
Fsus4
'cos they wan - na turn it on,
Bm7
Cm7
D
Eb
so their minds are soft and laz - y.
A
Bb
Well,

F♯m7
Gm7
Dadd9
E♭add9
Hey,
A
B♭
hey, give 'em what they want. If lust and hate is the Can-
F♯m7
Gm7
D
E♭
dy, if blood and love taste so sweet, then
A
B♭
we give 'em what they want.

A/C♯
D
B♭/D
E♭
So their eyes are growing haz - y
Esus4
Fsus4
'cos they wan - na turn it on,
Bm7
D
to Coda
Cm7
E♭
so their minds are soft and laz - y. Well,
Bm
A
Bm
A
Cm
B♭
Cm
B♭
who,
who,

Bm
Cm
A
B♭
D
E♭
who,
who,
do you want to blame?
D.S. al Coda
Coda
Well,
who,
who,
who,
do you want to blame?

Tolerance

MERCHANT

C Db F G C Db

vio - lence. A loud break-ing sound in the night is made.
fear - ing is the hate that pa-rades up and down our streets,

F Gb 1. Am Bbm G Ab Am Bbm

Hear it grow, hear it fade.

2. Am Bbm G5 Ab5

com-ing with-in bounds

A5 Bb5

and with-in reach.

Fmaj7
Cadd9
G♭maj7
D♭add9
Now, in - side the place we hide a - way,
melody
p

Fmaj7
G♭maj7
we hear it near and hope it turns a -

Cadd9
G5
D♭add9
A♭5
way. Turn a - way...
melody
sub.f

Am C/E Am
Bbm Db/F Bbm

mf

There's some - thing seeth - ing in the air we're breath - ing. We learn slash and burn is the me-thod to use.

We're o - ver - pow - ered. We kneel, we cower we co - ver our heads. Feel the threat of blows that will come

C F
Db Gb

C 1. F Am
Db Gb Bbm

Set a flame, burn it new.

2.
F
Gb
Am
Bbm
G5
Ab5
and the dam-age that will be done
A5
Bb5
in its wake.
Fmaj7
Gbmaj7
Cadd9
Dbadd9
Now, in-side this place we hide a-way,
melody
Fmaj7
Gbmaj7
we hear it near al-though it's miles a-
we hear it near and hope it turns a-

Cadd9
Dbadd9
Fmaj7
Gbmaj7
way.
way.
We hear it near and
hope it turns a - way.
Turn a -
melody
sub. f
1. G5
Ab5
to next strain
way...
Fine
G5
Ab5
A5
Bb5
way...

Am
B♭m
C/E
D♭/F
Am
B♭m
C
D♭
F
G♭
C
D♭
F
G♭
Am
B♭m
f
Am
B♭m
C/E
D♭/F
Am
B♭m
C
D♭
This house divided, we live inside it.
mf
F
G♭
C
D♭
F
G♭
Am
B♭m
Hate's dwell-ing place is be-hind our door in fit-ful nights. Hear it walk the

G5
A♭5
A5
B♭5
floor and hear it rave as it
moans and drags a - long its ball and chain, as it
moves through this house it can't es - cape.
Fmaj7
G♭maj7
Cadd9
D♭add9
D.S. al Fine
sub. p

If You Intend

MERCHANT

Moderately, with a steady beat

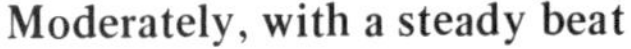

G
Ab
Gmaj7/F♯
Abmaj7/G
G6/E
Ab6/F
you in - tend to live a - gain, o - pen your eyes
(2.) you in - tend to live a - gain, then take the out -
mf
Bm/D
Cm/Eb
Cadd9
Dbadd9
and don't pre - tend you're feel - ing there's
stretched hand of one who needs you. It's
Dsus4
Ebsus4
G
Ab
no - thing worth be - liev - ing. God, if you per - sist you'll
been so long, we've missed you. Why do you in - tend to

Gmaj7/F♯
A♭/G
G6/E
A♭6/F
Bm/D
Cm/E♭
die like this, and with - er in the midst of your
speed your end? Lie in the dark and let your limbs
Cadd9
D♭add9
first sea - son, cut down with no
grow weak - er, sink - ing low then
D
E♭
C/G
D♭/A♭
D/F♯
E♭/G
C/E
D♭/F
D
E♭
rea - son.
deep - er.
How
C
D♭
D6/B
E♭6/C
D/A
E♭/B♭
G5
A♭5
Cmaj7/B
D♭maj7/C
D/A
E♭/B♭
D
E♭
can you be

Cmaj7/B
D/A
D
G5
Db♭maj7/C
E♭/B♭
E♭
A♭5
so near and not see
G5/F♯
G5/D
A♭5/G
A♭5/E♭
1.
2.
ev - ery - thing?
2. If
Em
D6
Fm
E♭5
Feel what might be.
sub. p
simile
See what

D6
E♭6
Am
B♭m
I see.
A-gain and a-gain and a-gain
and a-gain say you don't.
A-gain and a-gain and a-gain and a-gain say you
don't.
You say you don't, but you
cresc.

G
Gmaj7/F♯
G6/E
Bm/D
A♭
A♭maj7/G
A♭6/F
Cm/E♭
will.
mf
Instrumental solo
Cadd9
D♭add9
D
E♭
You say you don't, but you
C/G
D/F♯
C/E
D
C
D6/B
D/A
G5
D♭/A♭
E♭/G
D♭/F
E♭
D♭
E♭6/C
E♭/B♭
A♭5
will. How can you be
C/G
D/F♯
C/E
D
C
D6/B
D/A
G
D♭/A♭
E♭/G
D♭/F
E♭
D♭
E♭6/C
E♭/B♭
A♭
so near and not see?

I'm Not The Man

Merchant

Cmaj7
Dbmaj7
D5
Eb
Em
Fm
His eyes have gone a - way, es - cap - ing o - ver time.
Cmaj7
Dbmaj7
D5
Eb5
Em
Fm
D5
Eb5
He rules a crowd - ed na - tion in - side his mind.
G5 Cmaj7(no3)/B Em Cmaj7(no3)/B Cadd9
Ab5 Dbmaj7(no3)/C Fm Dbmaj7(no3)/C Dbadd9
2. He knows that
mf
Em
Fm
Cmaj7
Db5
D5
Eb5
Em
Fm
night like his hand. He knows ev - ery move he made.
(3.) day he was tried no wit - ness tes - ti - fied.
p

Cmaj7
Db maj7
D5
Eb5
Em
Fm
Late shift, the bell that rang, a time card won't fade.
No - thing but e - vi - dence, not hard to fal - si - fy.
Ten - oh - five his truck pulled home. Ten - oh - five he climbed the stair,
His own con - fes - sion was a pros - e - cut - or's prize,
a - bout the time he was ac - cused of be - ing there.
made up of fear, of rage and of out - right lies.
G5
Cmaj7(no3)/B
Cadd9
Ab5
Db maj7(no3)/C
Db add9
To Coda
But I'm not the man. He goes free as I
But I'm not the man. He goes free as the

G D/F♯ G C G D/F♯

A♭ E♭/G A♭ D♭ A♭ E♭/G

wait on the row for the man to test_ the rope he'll

f

G C G bass B bass

A♭ D♭ A♭♭bass Cbass

slip a - round_ my throat...____ and si - lence____

Em

Fm

D.S. al Coda 𝄋

me. 3. (𝄋) On the

p

Coda
G
D/F♯
C
Ab
Eb/G
Db
candle vig - il glows,
as they burn my clothes.
f
Gbass
Bbass
Em
Abbass
Cbass
Fm
As the crowd cries,
"Hang him slow!" and I feel my blood go cold,
Cmaj7
D5
Dbmaj7
Eb5
he goes free.
p

Cmaj7 D♭maj7 D5 E♭ Em Fm Cmaj7 D♭maj7
Call out the K K K,— they're wild af - ter me.— And with that fren - zied look of
D5 E♭5 Em Fm Cmaj7 D♭maj7 D5 E♭ Em Fm
half - de - men - ted zeal,— they'd love to serve— me up— my fi - nal meal.
Cmaj7 D♭maj7 D5 E♭ Em Fm Cmaj7 D♭maj7 D5 E♭5 Em Fm
Who'll read my—— fi - nal rite
pp
Cmaj7 D♭maj7 D5 E♭5 Em Fm Cmaj7 D♭maj7 D5 E♭5 Em Fm
and hear my—— last ap - peal?— Who struck this de-vil's deal?
ritard.

Jezebel

MERCHANT

A
G
A
B♭
A♭
B♭
care - ful - ly build - ing the mask I was wear - ing
G
A
Bm
A♭
B♭
Cm
for two years, swear - ing I'd tear it off.
A
B♭
I've sat in the dark ex - plain - ing
Bm
A
G
Cm
B♭
A♭
to my - self that I'm strain - ing too hard for feel -

A
G
A
B♭
A♭
B♭
ings
I ought to find
eas - i -
Bm
A
Cm
B♭
ly.
Called my - self Je - ze - bel.
Gmaj7
A♭maj7
to Coda
Somewhat faster, with a driving beat
I don't be - lieve.
Be -
D/F♯
Gadd9
Asus4
E♭/G
A♭add9
B♭sus4
fore I say that the vows we made weigh like a stone in my

Gadd9
A♭add9
heart.
D/F♯
E♭/G
Fam - i - ly is fam - i - ly,
Asus4
B♭sus4
don't let this tear us a - part.
Bm
Cm
Tempo I
D.S. al Coda
Coda
Somewhat faster, with a driving beat
I'm not say - ing I'm
re - plac - ing love for some o - ther world

D/F♯
Gadd9
Asus4
E♭/G
A♭add9
B♭sus4
to de - scribe the sa - cred tie that bound me to
Gadd9
D/F♯
Gadd9
A♭add9
E♭/G
A♭add9
you. I'm just say - ing we've mis - tak - en one
Asus4
Gadd9
D/F♯
B♭sus4
A♭add9
E♭/G
for thou - sands of words. And for that mis - take I've caused
Gadd9
Asus4
Bm
A♭add9
B♭sus4
Cm
you such pain that I damn that word.

D bass / E♭bass — B bass / C bass — A bass / B♭bass — G / A♭

I've no more ways to hide

Bm / Cm — D bass / E♭bass — B bass / C bass — A bass / B♭bass — G / A♭

that I'm a des - o - late

A / B♭ — G / A♭ — A♭9sus4 / B♭9sus4 — G / A♭

and emp - ty, hol - low place in - side.

D/F♯ / E♭/G — Gadd9 / A♭add — Asus4 / B♭sus4

Gadd9
Abadd9
D/F♯
Eb/G
Gadd9
Abadd9
I'm not say - ing I'm re - plac - ing love
Asus4
Bbsus4
Gadd9
Abadd9
D/F♯
Eb/G
for some o - ther word to de - scribe the sa-
Gadd9
Abadd9
Asus4
Bbsus4
Gadd9
Abadd9
cred tie that bound me to you.
D/F♯
Eb/G
Gadd9
Abadd9
I'm not say - ing love's a play - thing. No,

Asus4
Bbsus4
Gadd9
Abadd9
D/F♯
Eb/G
it's a pow-er-ful word, in-spired by
strong de-sire to bind my-self to you.
How I wish that we ne-ver had tried
to be man and his wife, to weave our lives in-to a

Additional Lyrics

2. You lie there, an innocent baby.
I feel like the thief who is raiding your home,
Entering and breaking and taking in every room.
I know your feelings are tender
And that inside you the embers still glow.
But I'm a shadow,
I'm only a bed of blackened coal.
Call myself Jezebel for wanting to leave.